The Berenstain Bears
Go Out to Eat

Dining out,
though quite a treat,
is a lot of work
for a bite to eat!

The Berenstain Bears
Go Out to Eat

Jan & Mike Berenstain

HARPER FESTIVAL
An Imprint of HarperCollins Publishers

The Berenstain Bears Go Out to Eat
Copyright © 2010 by Berenstain Bears, Inc.
HarperFestival® is an imprint of HarperCollins Publishers.
www.harpercollinschildrens.com
Library of Congress catalog card number: 2009922234
ISBN 978-0-06-057409-3 (trade bdg.)—ISBN 978-0-06-057393-5 (pbk.)
10 11 12 13 SCP 10 9 8 7 6 5 4 3
❖
First Edition

Everyone in the Bear family works hard. Brother and Sister go to school and do their homework every evening. They have chores to do around the house as well. Honey Bear's job is to be curious about everything and anything.

Papa makes good, solid furniture and sells it to the folks around Bear Country. All these jobs are important and take lots of hard work. But everyone knows Mama Bear works the hardest of all.

Mama does most of the cleaning, cooking, washing, and ironing. On top of that, she does a lot of the gardening and yard work. Taking care of Honey Bear is almost a full-time job in itself.

Of course, Papa and the cubs are grateful for all of Mama's hard work.
They try to help her out as much as possible. Every night they do the dishes
after dinner so Mama can rest and watch the evening news on TV.
But sometimes they like to do something extra special for Mama.

One evening when Mama was very tired after a long, hard day, Brother and Sister whispered something in Papa's ear.

"Hmm!" said Papa, smiling. "A very good idea."

"My dear," he said, turning to Mama, "get your hat and shawl. We are all going out to eat at the Bear Country Grill. It's time you had a night off."

"Yay!" cried Brother and Sister.

"Yay!" said Honey.

Mama smiled. "How nice! We haven't been out to eat in a long time."

It was Friday evening and everyone in Bear Country seemed to be out and about. The highway was jammed with traffic. When the family arrived at the restaurant, there was a crowd of customers waiting to get in.

PARK

Papa dropped off Mama outside the restaurant while he looked for a parking spot. The lot was almost full and Papa had to drive around and around before he found a spot right at the back of the restaurant.

"There will be a wait of about half an hour," Mama said, when Papa and the cubs joined her.

"A whole half an hour!" said Sister.

"That's nearly forever," complained Brother. "I'm so hungry!"

"I know what," said Papa. "Mama, why don't you stay here while I take the cubs for a walk?" Papa didn't really want to stand around waiting himself.

"A fine idea," agreed Mama, who thought relaxing on a bench for a little while sounded quite nice.

Papa and the cubs set off toward a little duck pond on the far side of the parking lot. They saw a mother duck with ducklings. Papa had some crackers in his pocket and the cubs had a fine time feeding the ducks.

When the crackers were gone, they said good-bye to the ducks and headed back to the restaurant. By then, Mama was so relaxed she was nearly asleep.

"Let's play 'I Spy,'" suggested Papa. "I spy something pink."

"Sister's hair bow," said Brother.

"That was quick," said Papa.

"I'll think up a harder one," said Brother, staring into the distance. "Okay, I spy something . . ."

Just then, the restaurant hostess told them that their table was ready.

"To be continued," said Mama, sitting up and stretching, "after dinner."

"We're starving!" said Brother and Sister, grabbing some bread.

"Just a minute," said Mama. "I don't want you two filling up on bread. You won't eat your dinner."

"Aw, Mama!" said the cubs.

"No arguments, please!" said Mama. "This is my evening out and what I say goes." Mama cut each cub a slice of bread and then had the basket taken away.

"Yes, Mama," said the cubs.

Honey had a sippy cup of juice, but she wanted a big glass of water like everyone else. She leaned out of her high chair to grab one, but knocked the glass over instead. Water spilled everywhere.

"Oh, dear!" said Mama, trying to sop up the water with her napkin.

"You take it easy, Mama," said Papa, leaping up. "I'll get it!" But Papa's elbow knocked over his own water, too. With some help from their server, they managed to get it all cleaned up.

"Are you ready to order now?" their server asked.

As a matter of fact, they had been too busy to look at their menus. But now they were too hungry to wait any longer.

"I'll have a hamburger and french fries," said Brother.

"Me too," said Sister.

"Just a minute," said Mama. "The hamburger is okay, but not the fries. You both need some healthy vegetables. Two side orders of broccoli, please."

"Broccoli?!" said the cubs in disappointment.

"Remember," warned Mama, "this is my evening out."

"Yes, Mama," the cubs said.

Mama and Papa ordered their dinners along with something for Honey. Then they had to wait and wait and wait. Mama brought coloring books and crayons out of her bag. Mama was always prepared. The cubs colored away happily for a time. But the restaurant was very busy and they still had a long time to wait.

"Is my dinner ready yet?" Sister asked Papa.

"Just a minute," he said. "I'll find out." He put his hand up to his ear, pretending to be on the phone. "Hello? Is this the kitchen? Sister Bear wants to know if her dinner is ready yet. Okay, I'll tell her. They say it will be right out."

"Very funny," she said.

"Ha," said Brother.

But just then their server did arrive with a big tray full of steaming food. "You see? I told you," said Papa.

The whole family dug in hungrily.

"Manners, please!" said Mama. "Let's slow down a little."

Before long, almost everything was gone—except for the broccoli.

"I want to see every bit of that delicious broccoli eaten," said Mama. "It's chock-full of vitamins."

"Why do vitamins have to taste bad?" Brother grumbled, swallowing his broccoli with a gulp.

"If you eat your broccoli, you get dessert," said Papa.

"Hooray for dessert!" said the cubs.

Once the dinner plates were cleared away, everyone ordered vanilla ice cream with fresh blackberries.

"This makes up for the broccoli," said Brother.

"That's for sure!" agreed Sister.

"Sure!" said Honey.

After they finished eating, Papa paid the bill and they all said good-bye to their server and the hostess. It was dark out now, and everything looked different.

"Where did we park?" Papa asked, looking around.

"I spy something red," said Brother.

"It's our car!" said Sister, pointing it out.

"I enjoyed going out to eat," said Mama as they put Honey in her car seat. "It was just what I needed after a long, hard day!"

"Do you know what the best part of going out to eat is?" asked Brother.

"Dessert?" guessed Sister.

"Hamburgers?" suggested Papa.

"No," said Brother. "It's no dishes to clean up afterwards."

"That's for sure!" they all agreed as they pulled out onto the highway and headed for home.

"Sure!" said Honey.